A collection of positive affirmations and companion to the bestselling I Am books

WHO I AM

Words I Tell Myself

BY SUSAN VERDE · ART BY PETER H. REYNOLDS

Abrams Books for Young Readers · New York

The illustrations in this book were created using traditional and digital inks, gouache, watercolor, and tea.

Library of Congress Control Number 2022952138

ISBN 978-1-4197-7091-3

Text © 2023 Susan Verde
Illustrations © Peter H. Reynolds
Book design by Natalie Padberg Bartoo

The illustrations in this book have been previously published.

Printed and bound in China
10 9 8 7 6 5 4 3 2 1

Abrams Books for Young Readers are available at special discounts when purchased in quantity for premiums
and promotions as well as fundraising or educational use. Special editions can also be created to specification.
For details, contact specialsales@abramsbooks.com or the address below.

Abrams® is a registered trademark of Harry N. Abrams, Inc.

ABRAMS The Art of Books
195 Broadway, New York, NY 10007
abramsbooks.com

To all you readers
speaking to yourselves
with love and kindness.
You've got this!

—S.V.

To Mary Pat Kelly
and Shirah who
both journey with
brave hearts.

—P.H.R.

Author's Note

We all have rough days, tough moments, times when we forget how fantastic we are and only see what we think is wrong. Sometimes, when we feel upset or disappointed by our mistakes and our challenges and we focus on the negative, the voice in our mind tells us things that are hurtful and unkind, and we feel even worse. Luckily, we can talk back to that unkind voice. We can find the voice that is true and supportive. We can find the words that lift us up, that keep us going and loving who we are. Those words are called **positive affirmations**: statements that are positive and supportive and true about YOU.

That is what this book is filled with: positive affirmations that tell you who you really are. *Who I Am* is meant to be a book you can return to over and over when you need it. Pulling lessons from all of the I Am series, it is a guide to help you say things to yourself that remind you of how wonderful you are, that help you speak to yourself with gentle kindness.

These are words you can say at any time. Maybe you can start the day with them while looking in the mirror. Maybe you can say them in your classroom with your classmates and teachers. Maybe you can write some on a piece of paper to carry in your pocket. And you can always say them silently in your head, whenever you need to, wherever you are. Even if it feels funny at first, think of what you would tell your best friend, and then tell yourself the same thing. The more you practice, the easier it becomes to speak to yourself with love, compassion, and kindness, and the better you will feel. You can encourage your friends to say these words, too.

If you are a teacher, caregiver, parent, or other adult, this book is for you to use with the kids in your life. You can pull it out anytime to help guide them. You can read it all at once or choose one affirmation each day, week, or month. You can say them first thing in the morning or just before bed. There is no right or wrong. And please don't forget to use them on yourself as well. Whoever you are, I encourage all of you to come up with more of your own positive affirmations—and add them to the ones in this book.

You are smart, kind, caring, beautiful humans, always learning and growing. You are goodness and friendship. You are important. You are love and peace and courage and so much more. Remind yourself every day that this is who you are.

Sometimes when I find myself struggling
or feeling down or discouraged,
my mind tells me words that are not loving or kind.

These words can get loud.

They can make me think for just a moment:
There is something missing in me,
something wrong with me.
That I *am* those words.

But these words are not what's true,
are not my potential,
my greatness.

Instead of believing them,
I can pause
and breathe deeply
and take the time
to find my *own* words that are true.

And when I say them to myself,
the other voice gets quiet,
and I hear only me,
taking care of me,
loving me.

It's with *these* words that
I am describing the real me.
With these words, I know
who I am.

When I have feelings
of sadness
or anger
or worry,

my mind might tell me,
It's wrong to have those feelings.

But I can tell myself:

I am human.
I am allowed to feel.
I am supposed to feel.

My mind might tell me,
Don't share your worries.

But I can tell myself:

Everyone has worries,
and they are okay to talk about.

My mind might tell me,
I will always feel this way.

But I can tell myself:

This feeling will pass.
Nothing is forever.

My mind might tell me,
I shouldn't make a mistake.

But I can tell myself:

I am always learning.
Mistakes are how I grow.

My mind might tell me,
I failed.

But I can tell myself:

I am brave.
I have the courage to try.
There is no such thing as failure,
I just haven't gotten there YET.

My mind might tell me,
I can't.

But I can tell myself:

Yes, I can!

When the unkind voice
gets loud and I feel down,
I can tell myself:

I am enough.
In this world, I matter.

I can tell myself:

I am unique.
That is what makes me
beautiful and miraculous.

I can tell myself:

I am thoughtfulness.
My heart is full of compassion.

I can tell myself:

I am kindness.
I make a difference.

I can silence the voice
that is not the truth,
anytime,
anywhere,

when I speak to myself
with encouragement
and love.

These are the words that are the *real* me.

This is who I am.

All of us can *choose*
the words we tell ourselves.
We can pick the ones that remind us
of our own goodness.
And our effort.
And our importance.

These are the words that are the *real* us.
And when we use them,
we know:

THIS

is who we are.

There are so many wonderful things you can say about YOU!
Now try creating your own positive affirmations.

WHO I AM...